Written by Emily Gale

Illustrated by Mike Byrne

This edition published by Parragon in 2011

Parragon
Queen Street House
4 Queen Street
Bath BA1 1HE, UK

ISBN 978-1-4454-5766-6

Printed in China

JUST JOSIE

and the perfect day

PaRragon

Bath • New York • Singapore • Hong Kong • Cologne • Delhi
Melbourne • Amsterdam • Johannesburg • Auckland • Shenzhen

This is 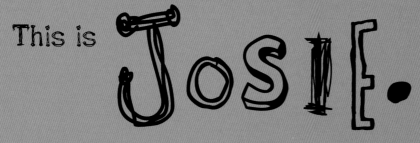 **JOSIE.**

Her full name is
JOSEPHINE EMILY
but everyone
just calls her Josie.

She loves rainbows,
clip-clop shoes
and her little sister Lily

(when Lily's being good).

Lily

Josie

Josie wears a different colour every day.
but on special days she dresses like a rainbow.
Josie has drawn a picture of tomorrow.
It's going to be the bestest most

perfect day ever!

ONE YEAR OLDER!

This is the biggest I've ever been. Now I can do grown-up things like:

CLIMB MOUNTAINS

WEAR CLIP-CLOP SHOES

AND GO TO BED LATE!

Now all Josie needs is **perfect** weather. . . .

But then it all goes **WRONG!**

It's not fair!

"I promised my friends the most superlicious garden party.

Rain is
NOT
part of my
BIG Idea.

Rain is the
WORST
thing EVER!"

DEEP BREATH
COUNT TO TEN
JOSIE'S GOT A
BIG IDEA AGAIN.

"I'm not letting nasty rain spoil my perfect day."

Josie remembers where rain comes from. Clouds.
"I'll just move them!"

But even with ALL of her family blowing really hard from the very top of the house. they can't make them budge.

The
rain
keeps
falling.

Then Josie remembers her manners.
"I know what will work."
says Josie. "I'm going to my
quiet place to speak to the
rain all by myself."

Hello rain.
it's me. Josie.
Please can
you go away.

Nothing happens. except the rain. which keeps on happening.

DEEP BREATH COUNT TO TEN. JOSIE'S GOT A BIG IDEA AGAIN.

"If everything else is perfect. this can still be a perfect day."

NUMBER ONE JOB my hair.

It takes a long time but finally Josie's hair is

perfect.

NUMBER TWO:
my party clothes.

Because Josie is in such a hurry it takes three goes to get her Mum's clip-clop shoes on the right feet.

clip
clop

clip
clop

ragh!

ragh!

Then she has a big job telling Lily she can't come to her party as a dinosaur.

At last Josie looks **perfect**,
just like a rainbow.

"Red and yellow and pink
and green, purple
and orange
and blue.
I can sing
a rainbow too!"

Josie's new Big Idea
is going well.

UNTIL...

BANG!

BANG! BANG!

The beautiful balloons start
popping.
Gran drops the jellies
on the floor.

splat!

Splat!

splat!

Lily starts crying because she hates **LOUD** noises.

waah!
waah!
waah!

And then the telephone rings. . . again, and again. **and again.** Mum has some bad news.

ALL of Josie's friends have chicken pox!

Finally the doorbell rings and Josie's happy that at least one of her friends has made sure not to get ill.

IT'S ZAC from next door.

Just when Josie thought that all the WORST things had already happened.

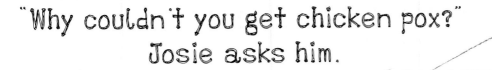
"Why couldn't you get chicken pox?"
Josie asks him.

And Mum tells Josie off. She tells her off on Josie's special day and she has to say sorry to Zac.

"It's not fair!"
shouts Josie.

That's it. Josie's
OLD BIG IDEA
and her
NEW BIG IDEA
are completely
RUINED.

She gets Duck
and sits in
the corner.

She DOESN'T WANT any presents.

(Not even that
great big one
over there.)

She DOESN'T WANT to play any games.

(Not even pin the clip-clop shoes on the princess.)

And she DOESN'T WANT any cake.

(Not even if it's made of chocolate.)

"This is the WORST day ever!" Josie says.

"The balloons all popped, the jellies went **splat!** Lily cried – a lot. The only person who came to my party just wiped a bogie on the cat and as if that wasn't bad enough: IT'S RAINING!"

She thinks she's in trouble but then Mum smiles and tells her to look out of the window.

Josie can't believe her eyes.

The yellowiest sunshine. . .

the bluest sky. . .

and the most

beautiful

rainbow anyone's

ever seen.

She grabs Lily's hand
and runs outside.

"Here I am on this **perfect** day,

with my very own rainbow...

my best and favourite party clothes...

Mum's clip-clop shoes...

a very chocolatey cake...

And it's even nice to
have Zac here, too.

Rainbows bring out the best in everyone!"